CAPTAIN CAT

Goes to Mars

by Emma J. Virján

Ready-to-Read

Simon Spotlight
New York London Toronto Sydney New Delhi

For Emma, my goddaughter

SIMON SPOTLIGHT
An imprint of Simon & Schuster Children's Publishing Division
1230 Avenue of the Americas, New York, New York 10020
This Simon Spotlight edition May 2022
Copyright © 2022 by Emma J. Virján
For information about special discounts for bulk purchases, please contact Simon &
Schuster Special Sales at 1-866-506-1949 or business@simonandschuster.com.
Manufactured in the United States of America 0322 LAK
10 9 8 7 6 5 4 3 2 1
Library of Congress Cataloging-in-Publication Data
Names: Virján, Emma J., author, illustrator.
Title: Captain Cat goes to Mars / by Emma Virján.
Description: New York : Simon Spotlight, 2022. | Series: Captain Cat |
Summary: Captain Cat and Pilot Matt fly their spaceship off to Mars,
where they make new friends among the stars.
Identifiers: LCCN 2021041130 | ISBN 9781534495739 (paperback) | ISBN
9781534495746 (hardcover) | ISBN 9781534495753 (ebook)
Subjects: CYAC: Stories in rhyme. | Cats—Fiction. | Mars
(Planet)—Fiction. | Friendship—Fiction. | LCGFT: Stories in rhyme. | Picture books.
Classification: LCC PZ8.3.V732 Cap 2022 | DDC [E]—dc23
LC record available at https://lccn.loc.gov/2021041130

Captain Cat and Pilot Matt are building a spaceship.

They hammer, drill,

and drip.

Then they scrub, dry,

and zip.

The seat belts click.

The engines roar.

Look at Captain Cat and Pilot Matt soar.

They wave to Earth,
twirl through the stars,
whoosh by the moon,
and head straight for
Mars.

They land with a thud,

then take a huge leap.

They hear three noises:
blip, bloop, and beep.

Hello! I am Captain Cat, and this is Pilot Matt.

They all become friends
and start to explore.

They see a crater,

rover, dust, and more.

Boil.

Plop.

Sip.

Whoosh.

Wobble.

Tip.

Zoof, Zeff, and Zatt
know what to do.

They pound and drill,
then use red glue.

It is time to wave goodbye to their friends Zoof, Zeff, and Zatt.

Surprise!
Look who is joining
Captain Cat and
Pilot Matt!